Hi, All You Rabbits

By Carl Memling

Pictures by Myra McGee

Parents' Magazine Press ◆ New York

HI, ALL YOU RABBITS.
WHAT DO YOU DO?

We hop and stop.
Hop and stop.
Hop and stop.
That's what all rabbits do.

And we thump like this.

HI, ALL YOU DUCKS.
WHAT DO YOU DO?

We quack and we paddle.
Quack and paddle.
Quack and paddle.
That's what all ducks do.

I'm eating.

HI, ALL YOU HORSES.
WHAT DO YOU DO?

We trot and we gallop.

Trot, trot, trot, trot.

Gallop and gallop.

That's what all horses do.

And we go, neigh, neigh.

Hi, all you rabbits
and all you ducks
and all you horses.
What do all of you do?

Hop and stop. Hop and stop.

Quack, quack. Quack, quack.

We trot and we gallop.

Neigh. Neigh.

HI, ALL YOU BIRDS.
WHAT DO YOU DO?

We sing and we fly.
We sing, sing, sing.
We fly, fly, fly.
That's what all birds do.

And nests! We sit in nests.

HI, ALL YOU PIGS.
WHAT DO YOU DO?

We oink and we wallow.
   We wallow, wallow, wallow.
   We oink, oink, oink.
That's what all pigs do.

Mmmmm, mud. We wallow in mud. Mmmmmm.

HI, ALL YOU COWS.
WHAT DO YOU DO?

We moo and we chew.

   We moo, moo, moo.

   We chew and chew and chew.

That's what all cows do.

We not only chew and moo. We give milk, too.

Hi, all you birds
and all you pigs
and all you cows.
What do all of you do?

We fly, fly, fly.
Oink, oink, oink.
We moo and we chew.
We give milk, too.

HI, ALL YOU CHICKS.
WHAT DO YOU DO?

We go, peep, and we peck.
Peep, peep, peep.
Peck, peck, peck.
That's what all chicks do.

Peep, peep. Wait for me.

HI, ALL YOU SHEEP.
WHAT DO YOU DO?

We get shorn and we ba-a-a.
Ba-a-a, ba-a-a, ba-a-a.
That's what all sheep do.

Yes, sir.
Yes, sir.
That's our wool.

HI, ALL YOU CATS.
WHAT DO YOU DO?

We rub and we purr.

Rub and purr.

Rub and purr.

That's what all cats do.

And meow! We meow, too.

HI, ALL YOU PUPS.
WHAT DO YOU DO?

We run and bark.
Run and bark.
Run and bark.
Yip, yip, yip.
That's what all pups do.

Yip, yip, a bone!

Hi, all you chicks
    and all you sheep
    and all you cats
    and all you pups.
What do all of you do?

Peep, peep.
Ba-a-a, ba-a-a.
Purr, purr.
Yip, yip, yip.

NOW WE KNOW WHAT RABBITS DO
and what ducks do
and what horses do
and what birds do
and what pigs do
and what cows do
and what chicks do
and what sheep do
and what cats do
and what pups do.

BUT—

HI, ALL YOU BOYS AND GIRLS.
WHAT DO YOU DO?

Everything!
Everything!
Just about
everything!

THAT'S...

WHAT BOYS AND GIRLS DO!

CARL MEMLING, until his death in 1969, was chairman of the Publications Division of the Bank Street College of Education. He was managing editor of the "Bank Street Readers" series published in 1964, and senior editor of Bank Street's "Early Childhood Discovery Materials."

Mr. Memling was the author of many delightful books for young children, including *Seals for Sale*, *Gift Bear for the King* and *The Dennis the Menace Storybook*. Three of his books soon to be published are *Ride, Willy, Ride*, *The Boy Went up the Mountain*, and *What's in the Dark?*

MYRA McGEE lives in a rural area of New York State where she and her husband both work in a barn studio and where Mrs. McGee can watch farm animals at work and at play from her kitchen window.

A Phi Beta Kappa graduate of Connecticut College for Women, Mrs. McGee is the mother of four children as well as both a writer and illustrator. Her books for young readers include *What is Your Favorite Smell, My Dear?*, *What is Your Favorite Thing to Touch?*, *What is Your Favorite Thing to See?* and *What is Your Favorite Thing to Hear?*